Disney

Anna & Elsa

The Polar Bear Piper

Disney

Anna & Elsa

The Polar Bear Piper

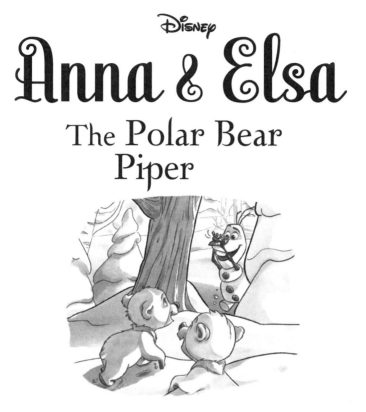

By Erica David
Illustrated by Bill Robinson,
Manuela Razzi, Francesco Legramandi,
and Gabriella Matta

Random House 🏠 New York

Chapter 1

It was an unseasonably warm day in the kingdom of Arendelle. Princess Anna tilted her head to the sky and sighed, enjoying the feel of the sun's rays on her arms and face. She was making her way from the royal palace to the town square. Today was the day she had agreed to host story time for all the village children.

Anna loved to read. She was eager to share her love of books with the smallest citizens of Arendelle. She was especially pleased that it would be warm enough to hold story time outside.

Anna strolled past the shops lining the cobblestone street. She passed Tilda's bakery on the corner. She waved to Leander, who ran the village laundry. He was hanging linens on a clothesline to dry. As usual, he was humming a lively tune. Finally, she reached the busy town square. She smiled when she saw such a large group waiting for her, gathered around the base of the clock tower. It seemed as if the children of Arendelle were looking forward to story time just as much as she was!

"Princess Anna! Princess Anna!" The children clapped and cried out in excitement when they saw the princess approaching.

"Hello, little ones," Anna said kindly. She pulled a large blanket from her knapsack and spread it on the ground. "Gather round now. We'll begin story time as soon as everyone finds a seat."

Anna waited patiently for each child to find a spot on the blanket. Just as she was about to pull her book from her bag, she heard someone shout, "Wait for me!"

It was Olaf, running toward them at full speed.

"Come to join us for story time, Olaf?" Anna asked.

"Oh, yes! I love stories!" Olaf said. "Do we have time for a warm hug first?"

Anna giggled and held out her arms. "We always have time for that!"

She watched as Olaf proceeded to dole out hugs to several of the children before taking a seat on the colorful blanket. When everyone had quieted down, she pulled out her book. "Today we'll be reading . . ." She paused for dramatic effect. *"The Pied Piper of Hamelin*!"

The children let out a chorus of oohs and aahs. Olaf turned to the little girl sitting beside him. "I've never heard this one before," he whispered, "but I think it might be my favorite!"

Anna raised the book high in the air so that all the children could see the picture on the cover. Then she carefully turned to the first page.

"'Once upon a time . . . ,'" she said, looking out at the sea of little faces. Everyone, including Olaf, was sitting in rapt attention. For the first time all day, it was silent in the town square. Anna smiled and continued to read.

The story was about a German town called Hamelin, which had become overrun by mischievous rats. The rodents ate all of the villagers' food. They left messy piles of trash in their wake. The king of Hamelin tried everything to get rid of the rats. Nothing he did seemed to work.

One day, a mysterious man with a magic flute appeared at the village gates. He promised to lead the rats out of town in exchange for a sack of gold. Then he began to play his flute. The rats, hypnotized by the music, formed a line behind the Pied Piper and followed him right out of town. Thanks to the Pied Piper's beautiful playing, the villagers of Hamelin were saved!

A round of applause broke out when Anna had finished the story. She stood and gave the children a playful bow. Olaf, meanwhile, was sitting stock-still on the blanket. His eyes were wide, his mouth agape.

"What did *you* think of the story, Olaf?" Anna asked.

Olaf jumped up from his seat and clapped his hands together with glee. "That . . . was . . . *wonderful*!" he shouted.

To Anna's surprise, Olaf took his carrot nose in both hands and pretended it was a magic flute. He marched and pranced around the blanket, using his carrot nose as a flute while he hummed a catchy tune. The children shrieked and giggled with delight. They got in line behind Olaf, just like the rats of Hamelin, and followed him

around the town square.

Anna was clapping in time to the beat when she suddenly felt her stomach rumble. "Come on, Olaf!" she called. "It's almost time for dinner! Let's head back to the palace and see what Elsa's been up to."

Anna and Olaf waved goodbye to the children, promising to read them a new story next week.

*

By the time Anna and Olaf reached the palace, the sun had already begun to set behind the North Mountain. With Olaf bouncing happily along beside her, Anna walked through the massive palace doors, across the Great Hall, and past the royal kitchen, stopping just outside the audience chamber. She was about to pull open the door when she heard Elsa calling them from down the hallway.

"Anna! Olaf!" Elsa waved and hurried over. "How was your day?"

"Oh, it was wonderful," Anna said. "We read *The Pied Piper of Hamelin,* and then Olaf started playing his nose like a flute. . . ."

Elsa laughed. "That sounds like fun! I can't wait to hear all about it. But as you can see, I haven't quite finished with the day's meetings."

Elsa opened the door and gestured to a line of villagers still waiting patiently for an audience with the queen. "Can we talk more at dinner?"

"Of course!" Anna said. She knew that meeting with the people of Arendelle was an important part of her sister's job. She looked around for Olaf, but he was already chatting with the villagers in line, telling them all about the Pied Piper.

Anna took the stairs two at a time and pushed open the heavy oak door to her room. After the day's excitement, it would be nice to have a few quiet moments to herself. She plopped down into a plush armchair and reached for her favorite book: an old and well-worn copy of *The Nansina Drude Files.*

Anna loved all stories, but she especially loved reading mysteries. As she flipped through the pages of her book, she wished that she had a case to work on, too—just like the brilliant detective Nansina Drude. But there wasn't much in Arendelle to investigate these days. The secret of Elsa's magic had already been revealed. Anna had figured out why she was missing some of her childhood memories. It seemed as if there wasn't much mystery left.

Just then, Anna heard a sharp rap on the door.

It was Elsa. She walked across the room and took a seat on the edge of Anna's bed. Her brow was furrowed.

"Anna," Elsa said in her most serious voice, "something mysterious is going on in Arendelle."

A mystery to solve! Anna sat up with a start. "What's happened?" she asked.

"It appears that someone has been stealing fish from the wharf," Elsa said. "And pies from the bakery, too."

Anna leaped from her chair and dashed

to the closet. "Oh, where is it?" she said to herself. "Aha! Here it is!"

Anna turned around, holding a notebook for writing down evidence. "Let's go!" she said. "I'm ready to investigate!"

"Not so fast," Elsa said with a smile. "You won't be solving any mysteries on an empty stomach."

Anna felt her stomach rumble again. "I *am* hungry," she admitted. She flashed Elsa a sheepish grin.

"Me too," Elsa said. "Let's go to dinner. We can start our investigation bright and early tomorrow morning."

Chapter 2

Early the next morning, Anna, Elsa, and Olaf set off for Tilda's bakery. Armed with her notebook and a knapsack for carrying evidence, Anna was eager to start working the case.

"I just can't imagine anyone stealing anything in Arendelle," she said with dismay. "Do you think it's possible that Tilda simply misplaced the pies?"

"I don't think so," Elsa said, shaking her head. "Tilda is a master baker. Besides, she's not really the forgetful type."

"That's true," Anna admitted. "It's puzzling."

Anna continued along the path, deep in thought about the mystery of the missing pies. When she reached the entrance to Tilda's bakery, however, she stopped short. The large wooden door was completely off its hinges. She could hear some kind of commotion coming from inside the shop.

"Hello?" Anna called, taking a few cautious steps forward. "Is anyone there?"

At the sound of Anna's voice, Tilda

came barreling out of the kitchen. She buried her face in her hands.

"Oh, Queen Elsa! Princess Anna!" Tilda cried. "Thank you for coming. It's my pies! They're . . . well, see for yourselves!"

Anna scanned the room. In the corner stood Tilda's icebox with its door ajar, revealing its empty shelves.

"There's more," Tilda said. "Look over there!" She pointed to a nearby windowsill, which was dotted with telltale drops of bright red pie filling.

Anna went over to inspect the evidence more closely. She fished her magnifying glass from her knapsack and squinted one eye, peering down at the pie filling. She drew the pattern of the pie splatter in her evidence notebook. Finally, she stuck her finger directly into the pie filling, then popped her finger straight into her mouth.

"Hmm . . . cherry," she said thoughtfully.

"Ooh, cherry!" Olaf said enthusiastically.

"Yes, cherry," Tilda wailed. "I made twelve cherry pies and left them to cool. But now they're gone! Who would do such a thing?"

"I don't know," Elsa said, gently taking Tilda's hand.

"Someone who likes cherry pies?" Olaf suggested innocently.

"No one could eat that many pies!" Tilda protested.

"One thing's for sure," Anna said. "Something very strange has happened here."

Tilda let out a sigh. "It's not just my shop, you know," she said. "Strange things have been going on all over the village. You should speak with Elin at the wharf. She's been having some trouble of her own, I hear."

"Thank you, Tilda," Elsa said with a reassuring smile. "And don't worry. We'll get to the bottom of this."

Anna, Elsa, and Olaf set off for the harbor at once. As soon as she set foot on the town dock, Anna saw that Elin, Arendelle's most experienced fisherwoman, was rushing toward them.

"Queen Elsa, Princess Anna," Elin said. "Thank goodness you're here."

"We heard there was something fishy going on at the wharf," Anna said.

"What's the trouble?" Elsa asked.

Elin clasped her hands together and cleared her throat. "As you both know, it's been unusually warm in Arendelle lately. All of the ice in the harbor has begun to thaw."

"Go on," Anna said, concentrating. Her pencil hovered just above her evidence notebook. She was poised to write

down whatever Elin might have to say.

"Our boats can sail freely in and around the harbor," Elin continued. "Our haul has been especially abundant. We've caught more fish than ever this year!"

Anna stopped writing. She raised an eyebrow and shot Elsa a quizzical look.

"Isn't that a *good* thing?" Elsa asked.

Elin chuckled. "It's a wonderful thing. Still, I couldn't help noticing that some of our fish have gone . . . *missing.*" She pointed to the grassy banks of the harbor. The ground was littered with hundreds and hundreds of fish bones.

Elsa gasped.

"Would you look at that?" Anna said, stunned. She made a quick note in her evidence notebook.

"Indeed," Elin said. "By the way, you might want to speak with Leander at the village laundry. I heard something odd has gone on over there, too."

They hadn't heard about any problems

at the laundry. Luckily, it was a quick walk from the wharf down to the edge of town. As they rounded a bend, Anna spied Kristoff and Sven in the distance. She put her fingers between her teeth and whistled.

Kristoff waved from across the clearing.

"Have you heard about all this mysterious mischief going on in Arendelle?" Kristoff asked. He was breathing heavily, and his cheeks were flushed from his jog across the glade.

"We certainly have," Anna said. "Elsa and I are going to crack this case wide open."

"What about me?" Olaf asked.

"With Olaf's help, of course." Anna smiled, patting his head.

"You know," Kristoff said, lowering his voice, "some of the ice harvesters are saying this could be the work of . . . *polar bears.*"

Anna couldn't believe what she was hearing.

"Polar bears?" Elsa said. "I don't think so. Polar bears live in the Arctic. That's much, much farther north."

Kristoff shrugged. "That's the rumor up at the frozen lake."

"Why don't you and Sven come with us to the village laundry?" Anna asked. "We

have to solve this mystery as soon as we can. We could definitely use some help!"

Kristoff and Sven were eager to lend a hand. Unfortunately, things weren't looking good at Leander's.

As she crossed the threshold of the village laundry, Anna could see clothes hanging willy-nilly from the rafters. There was water everywhere. Several of the washtubs were upside down and empty. And instead of humming his usual cheerful tune, Leander was on his hands and knees, scrubbing the floor.

"Queen Elsa, Princess Anna," Leander said with a shake of his head. "It's a mess."

Anna got right to work collecting evidence from the scene. While she looked around, a bedsheet slipped from the rafters and drifted down from the ceiling. It landed right on top of Olaf, covering his little snowman body completely.

"Guys!" Olaf shouted. "I can't see!" He ran around and around before bumping into Leander's knee and falling to the ground. "It's an eternal night!" he exclaimed, arms flailing.

Kristoff stepped forward and gently lifted the sheet from Olaf's head.

"Daylight!" Olaf laughed. He was bending down to brush himself off when he noticed something near his feet. "What are these?"

Anna stepped forward, drawing her magnifying glass from her knapsack. "Are those . . . animal tracks?" she asked.

Kristoff inhaled sharply and crossed his arms. "Those look like *bear* tracks to me."

"Oh! *Polar* bear tracks?" Olaf asked.

"I don't know," Anna said, shaking her head. "But this case just got a whole lot more interesting."

Chapter 3

Anna bent over and peered through her magnifying glass, her nose inches from the ground. She carefully inspected the muddy bear tracks. Then she began to follow them across the floor of Leander's laundry and out into the street.

Once outside, Anna gazed into the distance. It looked like the muddy tracks led across the clearing, deep into the forest, and straight out of town.

"Well, there's only one thing left to do now," Anna said. "Follow these tracks!"

Elsa was smiling at her.

"What?" Anna asked.

"I'm impressed," Elsa said.

"It's what Nansina Drude would do," Anna said. She turned to the rest of the group. "What do you say?"

"I'm in," Kristoff said, crossing his arms and rocking back on his heels. "This is exciting."

"Me too!" Olaf said. "I've always wanted to see a polar bear!"

Sven raised his hairy eyebrows and

jumped up and down on his hooves.

"Then it's settled," Elsa said with a laugh. "Anna, you lead the way!"

Anna and her friends followed the tracks across the clearing. As they neared the forest edge, Anna noticed something shiny and red on the ground.

"This looks like the remains of one of Tilda's pies!" she cried. She stuck her finger in the sugary-sweet syrup and popped her finger into her mouth. "And it's cherry! We're definitely on the right track!"

The group continued, following a dirt path that meandered through the trees. Moments later, Sven let out a loud whinny. He was standing next to a spruce tree, pointing with his snout at something tangled in the roots.

"What have you got there, buddy?" Kristoff said. He knelt down to inspect the roots more closely. "Looks like more fish bones and . . . a sweater?" He held up a large wool sweater by the sleeves. "You know, this might look pretty good on you, Sven."

Sven snorted his disapproval.

"May I see that?" Anna asked, taking a few steps forward. She slowly turned the sweater over in her hands. "This looks like it might have come from Leander's laundry."

She tossed the sweater into her evidence

knapsack. Then she collected some of the
discarded fish bones. She tossed those into
her pack, too.

"Those bones have quite an odor," Elsa
said.

"I know," Anna said, breathing through
her mouth. "But according to Nansina
Drude, it's important to collect all the

available evidence when you're hoping to solve a case."

As Anna and her friends walked deeper into the forest, the trees seemed to be growing taller. The foliage grew denser. Less and less daylight filtered through the lush canopy. The only sound was the crunching of leaves and gravel under the detective squad's feet.

"I was thinking," Elsa said, breaking the silence. "We should discuss what to do if we actually find a polar bear."

"Good idea, Elsa," Anna said. "Maybe we should run?"

"I don't think so," Kristoff said, shaking his head. "Polar bears are very fast. They could easily outrun us all. If we do see a polar bear, I think we should hide."

Anna and Elsa both nodded, but Olaf looked up in disbelief.

"Isn't it obvious?" he said. "We should make *friends* with the bears."

Anna stifled a laugh and caught Elsa's eye.

"I'm not sure that's a very good idea, Olaf," Elsa said.

"What do you mean?" Olaf asked. "Everybody knows that polar bears are fluffy and sweet! I bet they give excellent hugs!" He wrapped his stick arms around his body, hugging himself.

"Olaf," Kristoff said, "polar bears are ferocious and huge. Twice the size of Sven at least."

Sven puffed out his chest, trying to make his body appear larger. He snorted.

"Sorry, buddy," Kristoff said, patting Sven's head. "But it's true."

Just then, Anna heard a sound in the forest. "Shh!" she whispered, sticking her finger in the air. "Did you hear that?"

Anna and her friends lifted their heads and pricked their ears. There was another loud crack and a snap. Anna thought it sounded like tree limbs bending and breaking. As the sound got louder, she felt her arms break out in nervous goose bumps.

Suddenly, two polar bears tumbled into the path. They nipped and pawed at each other playfully. They turned somersaults.

They were wee little things, not much bigger than puppies. They were cubs.

Anna couldn't help smiling. These two little bears were *adorable*.

"Oh, see!" Olaf said sweetly. "Look how cute they are! I told you that polar bears would make great friends!"

Olaf skipped down the path, closer and closer to the cubs. Anna was about to warn him to slow down when she heard the sound of more tree limbs snapping and breaking. She looked to her left, just in time to see a huge polar bear poke its head out from between the trees.

"Uh-oh," Kristoff whispered. "That must be the mama."

The polar bear lumbered out of the woods and into the path, snarling. Then, to Anna's dismay, it reared back on its hind legs and let out a terrifying growl. Anna had to keep tilting her chin higher and higher to take in the bear's massive size. At full height, the polar bear stood more than ten feet tall.

"Elsa?" Anna whispered urgently. "Any ideas?"

Before Elsa could respond, the polar bear sprang forward, running toward the group at full speed. Anna was just about to shout *"Use your magic!"* when a cold gust of wind whipped past her face.

Anna turned to see Elsa standing with

her arms outstretched. A huge wall of ice was rising rapidly from the ground. The polar bear slid to a halt and dropped back down onto all fours. It was safely behind the wall of ice.

"Nice one, Elsa!" Kristoff shouted.

Anna let out a sigh of relief. But suddenly, the bear leaped forward again, crashing through the wall. Sparkling shards of ice littered the forest ground.

Elsa's face lit up in surprise.

"I guess polar bears are pretty used to crashing through ice and snow, huh?" Kristoff said.

The bear was charging now. Anna racked her brain. *Oh, what would Nansina*

Drude do? she thought desperately.

She had an idea. She pulled her evidence bag from her shoulder and tossed it high in the air, launching it right over the polar bear's head.

"What are you doing, Anna?" Kristoff asked.

"Just wait!" Anna whispered.

Sure enough, the massive polar bear caught a whiff of the fish bones stashed inside Anna's bag. The bear lifted its head and sniffed. Then it turned, following the smell of the food, leaving Anna and her friends just enough time to escape.

"Anna, that was genius!" Elsa said.

"Thanks, Elsa!" Anna said, still trying

to catch her breath. "Now let's get back to the palace!"

Anna and her friends let out a collective sigh of relief.

Chapter 4

"Well, now we know. All of this mischief in Arendelle is definitely being caused by . . . *polar bears.*"

Anna and her friends were sitting around a large table in the throne room, discussing how to solve their polar bear problem. Even though she had tossed her evidence knapsack into the woods, Anna still had her detective's notebook. She flipped through the pages, going back over the notes she had taken during the course of the day.

"Well, I am surprised," Elsa said, resting her hands flat on the table. "The Arctic is hundreds of miles away. I can't imagine how or why these polar bears ended up so far south, so far from their natural home."

"What should we do?" Kristoff asked. "How can we help them get back?"

"I'm not sure," Elsa said. "But right now, I need to alert the villagers in order to keep everyone informed and safe. Kai?"

Elsa summoned the royal handler, who had been standing by for instructions.

"Yes, Your Majesty?" Kai asked with a deep bow.

"Please tell the villagers that I will be giving an important speech in the town square this evening."

"Right away, Your Majesty," Kai said.

Elsa looked at the piles of notes stacked up and spread out on the table. "Anna," she said softly, "would you help me work on my speech?"

*

It was another unusually warm night, and the moon shone bright in the sky. Right on time, the villagers of Arendelle had gathered in the town square, lighting the way with lanterns and torches. They stood crowded together, shoulder to shoulder, eager to hear Elsa's speech.

Anna was standing next to her sister at the base of the clock tower. She knew that Elsa was waiting for the gossiping and whispering to die down. After a few moments, when the villagers still hadn't quieted, Anna put her fingers between her teeth and whistled loudly. Then Olaf, always eager to help, stepped forward, cupped his hands around his mouth, and shouted, "ATTENTION, PEOPLE OF ARENDELLE!"

The entire village snapped to attention.

"Thank you, Anna, Olaf," Elsa said, smiling. She took a step or two forward, clasped her hands together, and cleared her throat.

"People of Arendelle," Elsa began. "As you know, there has been some mysterious activity in our town lately. Tilda's pies were stolen from the bakery. Fish were taken from the wharf. And someone has been snatching clothes from the laundry."

The villagers murmured and nodded.

"My sister and I have been investigating the cause of this mischief all day," Elsa continued. "I can now confirm that polar bears are the cause of our troubles."

"Polar bears?" someone shouted.

"This far south?" cried another villager.

Elsa raised her hands to quiet the crowd. "It's surprising, I know. I'm not sure how they got to Arendelle. I'm not even sure why they're here. What I *do* know is that they seem to be hungry, because they've been eating everything in sight. That's why I'm issuing a royal decree. Everyone in the kingdom must lock up their food *and* their doors, at least until this polar bear problem is solved."

The square erupted in shouts of concern and confusion. No one in Arendelle had experienced anything quite like this before.

Just then, a booming voice rang through the crowd. "Your Majesty?"

Anna recognized him immediately. It was Hrödebert, flanked by his brothers Josef and Benja. They were three exceptional huntsmen who lived on the outskirts of town.

"Perhaps we should hunt these bears down and drive them out?" Hrödebert suggested.

A chorus of cheers rang out in support.

Elsa held up her hand once more. "These

polar bears are a long way from home. I don't think they mean us any harm. In fact, my sister and I are returning to the palace to continue our investigation. I believe that we can find a solution that will benefit all of us . . . *including* the bears."

Hrödebert gave a deferential bow and retreated with his brothers into the crowd. Anna was pleased to see that most of the villagers were nodding enthusiastically with respect and approval. She could tell that with Elsa in charge, the people of Arendelle felt safe.

Elsa turned from the crowd and reached for Anna's hand. "If we're going to solve this polar bear problem once and for all," she said, "we're going to have to learn

more about them. Ready for some more detective work?"

Anna smiled. "Whatever you need, Elsa."

Feeling confident, the sisters walked arm in arm back to the palace.

＊

Anna was sitting at a desk in her father's library, surrounded by piles and piles of books. She had been up all night, reading everything there was to read about polar bears. The more she and Elsa knew about them, Anna thought, the better able they would be to solve the case.

"It says here that polar bears are drawn to human food," Elsa reported.

She was holding up an old copy of *Jörgen's Polar Bear Digest.* "So with all of our food locked away, the bears will probably have no choice but to head home soon."

"I hope so," Anna said, rubbing her eyes. "But we still don't know what the bears were doing at the village laundry."

Elsa stretched her arms above her head and yawned. "That's true, but I don't think we're going to figure that out without some rest. I'm exhausted."

Anna closed the book she was reading and yawned, too. "You're probably right. Let's go to bed."

Just as Anna finished gathering up her notes and papers, the door to the library opened. Kai entered. "Your Majesties, news from town," he said. "When Tilda went to open her bakery this morning, she found the windows smashed."

"Oh, no," Anna said, slumping back down in her chair. She knew what that meant. Without available food, the bears had only grown bolder. The plan—to lock up all of the village food—had failed.

Chapter 5

By dawn, Anna and Elsa were standing in the doorway to Tilda's bakery. The sidewalk was littered with shards of glass from the broken windows. Several huge claw marks marred the shutters and walls.

"I guess it's more serious than we thought," Elsa said, wringing her hands.

Anna nodded. "I know. I think we

should head back to Leander's laundry and pick up the tracks there again. We can follow them deeper into the woods this time. See if we can find any more clues."

A look of concern spread across Elsa's face. "Don't you remember what happened last time?"

Anna thought back to the narrow escape she and her friends had made from the charging mama bear. She remembered how easily the bear had crashed through Elsa's magical ice wall. She recalled just how loud the polar bear's growl had been.

"Those tracks are our only lead," Anna said. She reached for her sister's hand and gave it a reassuring squeeze. "Don't worry, Elsa. I'll think of something."

Anna, Elsa, and Olaf stood outside Leander's laundry, waiting for Kristoff and Sven. Anna was pleased to see that Leander, still busy cleaning up after the polar bears, was at least back to humming his cheerful tune. When the boys were within shouting distance, Anna cupped her hands around her mouth and hollered, "Did you bring what I asked for?"

"Sure did!" Kristoff said, sidling up to the sisters. He placed his rucksack on the ground and began digging through it. He pulled out an ice pick and tossed it over his shoulder. He threw a coil of rope to the ground. Finally, he pulled out several silver pots and pans and raised them high over his head. "Ah, here we go!"

"I don't get it," Elsa said, confused. "What do we need these pots and pans for?"

Kristoff handed Anna a sauté pan and a wooden spoon, which Anna proceeded to bang together. The noise was so loud that Elsa immediately covered her ears with her hands.

"See?" Anna said, feeling pleased with herself. "We just bang these together. The noise should scare the bears away. Problem solved!"

"Oh, I get it!" Elsa said. "That's smart!"

Kristoff decided to join in the fun. He started banging two pots together, creating an earsplitting clang.

"Oh, that's so beautiful!" Olaf said, clapping his hands.

Anna laughed, but her ears were starting to ring. "All right, Kristoff. You can stop now!"

"Sorry about that," Kristoff said with a laugh, blushing. "Guess I got a little carried away." He handed out the rest of his cookware to Elsa and Olaf. "Everyone ready to go?"

"No time like the present!" Anna said.

Anna and her friends set off in the direction of the bear tracks once more. Every few feet, Kristoff and Elsa would bang their pots together, just in case the bears were nearby. Olaf giggled loudly every time he struck metal spatula to spoon. "This is great!" he said.

Meanwhile, as Anna walked deeper and deeper into the forest, she began to let her mind wander. What were these polar bears doing in Arendelle? Why had they come? And more importantly, why hadn't they returned home yet?

Lost in thought, Anna rounded a bend in the path and stopped short. She lifted her nose to the wind and sniffed. "What on earth is that smell?" she said.

Kristoff sniffed twice and doubled over. "Oh! That's awful! It smells like rotting food!"

"I think it's coming from over there,"

Elsa said, nodding her chin in the direction of a gap in the trees.

Anna followed the polar bear tracks farther down the path, through the gap in the trees and into a clearing. When she raised her head, she couldn't believe her eyes. In front of her towered a heaping pile of garbage.

"What *is* all that?" Kristoff asked.

Anna followed the tracks all the way to the base of the pile. She held her nose and crouched to get a better look. The garbage mound was full of rotting fish bones and food scraps. Anna saw tons of broken glass, torn and shredded bits of clothing, and pieces of seaweed and driftwood.

"Hey, isn't that Tilda's rolling pin?"

Elsa asked. She pointed to a wooden dowel sticking out from the side of the heap.

Anna placed her hands on the dowel and tugged. "It *is* Tilda's rolling pin," she said. "I guess now we know where all this garbage came from. The bears have clearly been bringing their stolen goods here for safekeeping."

"But why?" Olaf asked, covering his carrot nose.

"Who knows?" Elsa said, shaking her head. "If this is really the work of our polar bears, though, it looks as though they plan on staying in Arendelle for a while."

Kristoff was standing to the side of the trash heap with his sweater pulled up over his nose. Sven was walking backward, getting as far from the stinking pile as possible. Anna, meanwhile, passed Tilda's rolling pin from one hand to the other, thinking.

"Maybe," she said, "if we got rid of this trash heap, we could get rid of our polar bear problem, too?"

Kristoff shook his head doubtfully. "How are we going to manage that, Anna? This dump is enormous!"

Anna smiled and reached for Elsa's hand. "Come on. I think I might have an idea."

Chapter 6

Anna paced in front of her father's old wooden desk. Every few moments, she stopped to scribble furiously in her notebook and then chew the end of her pencil, lost in thought. After several minutes of this routine, Elsa walked over and placed a hand on Anna's shoulder.

"So?" Elsa asked. "Do you have a plan?"

Anna placed her notebook on the desk and took a deep breath. "All right, Elsa. Here's what I'm thinking. . . ."

Anna explained that to quickly clean up the garbage pile, they would need to enlist help from as many villagers as possible. She suggested that Elsa go to Tilda's bakery to recruit some pastry assistants. Kristoff should ride to the frozen lake and ask some of the ice harvesters to volunteer. Anna, meanwhile, would walk down to the wharf and ask Elin to spare five of the strongest, most capable fishermen.

"How does that sound?" Anna asked.

"I think that sounds like a good start," Elsa said, smiling.

Anna beamed. "Once we've assembled our teams, we'll meet back at the garbage pile and get to work," she said.

A few hours later, Anna was standing on top of the garbage mound with her hands on her hips, waiting. From one direction, she could see Elsa leading a team of bakers through the clearing. From the

other, Sven was pulling a huge sled filled with burly ice harvesters.

Anna flashed all of the workers a huge smile. She was moved that so many in the village were willing to lend a hand.

As Anna and her friends began sorting through the debris, though, she realized something. It would be a shame to let all of this junk go to waste. She turned to Elsa, who was working beside her, elbow-deep in a pile of fish bones.

"Elsa?" Anna said. "Do you think there's a way we could salvage some of this stuff?"

Elsa picked up a piece of piecrust and tossed it into a pile of food scraps. "That would be nice," she sighed. "But I'm afraid this might all be useless trash."

Anna stood up straight and gazed across the clearing. She noticed that a patch of beautiful daisies had sprouted near the edge of the trash mound. They were all taller, with much bigger blossoms than the other daises growing in the field farther away. Suddenly, Anna snapped her head in Elsa's direction and smiled. "Compost!" she shouted.

Elsa looked up from her work. "What do you mean, Anna?"

Anna picked up some fish bones and crouched next to her sister. "We can use a lot of this stuff to make compost! It will help the farmers of Arendelle grow much bigger crops. I read about composting in one of the books in Father's library!"

Elsa looked at the pile of garbage, her eyes growing wider. She turned back to Anna with renewed energy. "I bet we could find a use for all this broken glass and these old bottles, too!"

"We could give it to the town glass-blowers," Anna suggested.

"They could melt it down and use it to make new lanterns or chandeliers or . . . all sorts of things!" Elsa said.

Anna clapped her hands with glee. "All right, everyone!" she shouted. "New plan!"

She instructed the workers to sort the garbage into separate piles. One pile would contain all the fish bones and food scraps that could later be used to make rich compost for Arendelle's farmers. Another would contain broken glass and driftwood, things that could be melted down or repurposed by Arendelle's glass-blowers and craftspeople.

As the day progressed, more and more villagers showed up at the trash mound to volunteer. They brought shovels and wheelbarrows and other tools to help clean up the garbage and bring the reusable items back to town. By late afternoon, the last of the trash had been swept away. Anna and Elsa stood in the now-empty meadow,

admiring the results of their hard work.

"Well, it looks like those polar bears will have no choice now but to pack up and head back home," Elsa said. "I'm so proud of you, Anna."

"Couldn't have done it without you, Elsa," Anna said. She took one last look at the clearing. "I wish there was a way to thank all of the villagers, too. Without their help, this project would have taken forever!"

Elsa smiled and squeezed Anna's hand. "Maybe there is," she said. "Olaf, can you introduce me again?"

Olaf stepped forward, cupped his hands around his mouth, and shouted, "ATTEN-TION, PEOPLE OF ARENDELLE."

"Thanks," Elsa said, turning to address the crowd. "People of Arendelle, in appreciation of all of your help, and to celebrate the end of our polar bear problem, I'm inviting everyone to a party at the palace tomorrow night!"

The volunteers burst into cheers, clapping their hands and stomping their feet.

"Come on," Elsa said to her friends. "Let's go get everything ready."

*

The following evening, the palace grounds glittered with twinkling lights and colorful streamers. The party was in full swing. Anna looked around at the crowd of happy people laughing, eating, and dancing. She stifled a yawn. Who knew that solving mysteries could be so exhausting? She was looking forward to some peace and quiet. She smiled. Her face fell, however, when she looked up and saw Hrödebert the huntsman sprinting across the palace grounds.

"Queen Elsa! Queen Elsa!" Hrödebert cried. He was panting from his long run across town.

Elsa led him to a nearby chair to rest. "What is it, Hrödebert?" she asked.

Hrödebert took a moment to catch his breath. "I think we're going to have to do a lot more than clean up that garbage heap to get rid of these polar bears."

"Why do you say that?" Elsa asked.

"Because there's a whole family of them asleep in my shed!"

Chapter 7

"I can't believe we haven't solved this polar bear problem yet!" Anna said, slumping in the old armchair in her room.

Elsa took a seat next to Anna and patted her hand. "Don't worry. This is just a little setback. Cleaning up that garbage pile was a great idea! Look at all the good work you're doing."

Anna looked up at her sister and sighed.

"Thanks, Elsa. It's just . . . I thought cleaning up the trash mound in the forest was sure to do the trick."

Elsa walked across the room and picked up Anna's worn, leather-bound book from the nightstand. She placed it gently in her sister's lap. "I bet even Nansina Drude got stumped every once in a while," she said. "I wonder what she would do in a situation like this."

Anna blew the hair out of her face and got to her feet. She clasped her hands tightly behind her back. She began pacing the length of her room.

"If Nansina were here," Anna said, thinking, "she would probably say that we still don't have enough evidence to solve the case. What do we really know about polar bears, other than that they don't belong in Arendelle?"

"Maybe we should consult an expert," Elsa suggested. "You know, someone who knows more about animals than we do. Someone who could point out what we're missing."

Anna thought that was a good idea. She could use an expert's help. But where would she find a polar bear expert on such short notice?

"What about Grand Pabbie?" Elsa said suddenly. "Maybe he could shed some light on our polar bear problem."

"Yes!" Anna said. She was already rushing around her room to gather her things. She pulled on her shoes and tossed her cape over her shoulders. She had one foot out the door when Elsa called out after her.

"Hold on!" Elsa shouted. She sprang past Anna and down the hall. "Olaf and I are coming with you!"

Anna and Elsa found Olaf and hurried through the palace gates, across the village, and into the woods. Guided by the light of the stars, Anna brushed past tree limbs and branches. She skirted snowdrifts, searching for the trolls' valley.

"Wow!" Elsa said. She was a few paces behind Anna on the path. "Look at that!"

Anna turned her face to the sky. The

iridescent greens and shimmering blues of the northern lights swirled above.

"It's so beautiful," Olaf whispered.

It *was* beautiful, but Anna was eager to keep going. "Come on," she said, plunging ahead. "I think we're getting close."

As Anna continued scouting a path through the woods, she felt her foot slip on the edge of an embankment.

"Whooooa!" she cried. She flailed her arms to maintain her balance, but it was too late. She slid all the way down a steep ridge, landing with a thud on the stony ground.

"Anna! Are you okay? Where are you?" Elsa called from above.

"Down here!" Anna hollered. "I'm fine! Just be sure to watch your step!"

Anna stood, brushed herself off, and waited for Elsa and Olaf to make their way down the ridge. She was reaching for Elsa's hand when she saw several trolls roll from the shadows to greet them.

"Oh, the love experts!" Olaf cried cheerfully.

Anna smiled warmly and knelt down to speak to the trolls. "Is Grand Pabbie here?" she asked. "It's very important that we speak with him."

Just then, Grand Pabbie stepped out from behind a rock and ambled over to Anna and her friends.

"Hello, Your Majesty, Princess Anna,"

he said. "What brings you out here this evening?"

Elsa stepped forward and took Grand Pabbie's hands. "Polar bears have somehow made their way to Arendelle, Grand Pabbie," she said. "They've been raiding our shops and causing all kinds of mischief!"

"Polar bears, you say?" Grand Pabbie

said, raising his hairy eyebrows in surprise. "That *is* odd. Polar bears prefer extremely cold weather. It's unusual to find polar bears this far south."

Olaf stood with his eyes wide, his mouth open. "Colder than Arendelle, Grand Pabbie?"

"Yes, colder than Arendelle." Grand Pabbie chuckled softly. "Here, let me show you."

Grand Pabbie led Anna and her friends to a stony outcrop bathed in the light of the moon. Then he held up his hands. With a flick of his wrist, he began to conduct the northern lights. A picture formed in the sky.

"Polar bears spend most of their time

adrift on ice floes in the Arctic," Grand Pabbie said. With another flick of his wrist, the picture in the sky changed. Anna and Elsa could clearly see a polar bear floating on a large block of ice in the sea.

"But polar bears are migratory animals," Grand Pabbie continued. "They can travel long distances, depending on the weather. They are always in search of more ice and snow."

The picture in the sky changed again. This time Anna and Elsa could see a polar bear stepping off an ice floe onto a snow-covered stretch of land.

"What is puzzling about your situation," Grand Pabbie said, "is that polar bears almost always travel north, toward the ice caps. The only way they could have traveled south, all the way to Arendelle, is by mistake. How or why that happened, I'm afraid I cannot say."

Grand Pabbie flicked his wrist a final time and the picture in the sky disappeared. "I wish I could be of more assistance," he said. "Your polar bear problem is a true mystery."

Anna and Elsa stood up and thanked the troll for his kindness. Olaf, meanwhile, threw his stick arms around Grand Pabbie and gave him a warm hug.

Pabbie chuckled. "I wish you all the best of luck." With that, he rolled away and was gone.

As they hiked back through the forest, Anna thought long and hard about what Grand Pabbie had said. Maybe it really was a mystery. Maybe the case of the polar bears would never really be solved. Suddenly, she stopped. Turning to her right, she saw a gap in the trees. She knew what she needed to do.

"Go on ahead of me, Elsa," Anna said. "I'll catch up."

Chapter 8

Anna walked through the gap in the trees until she came to the edge of a tall bluff overlooking the fjord. She gazed at the wharf below. She watched as the moonlight danced on the village rooftops. This was one of Anna's favorite places in all of Arendelle. It was quiet and peaceful. She came here whenever she needed time to just sit and *think*.

Anna took a seat on the ground, resting her back against the smooth bark of an ancient tree. She tucked her feet beneath her and smoothed her skirt. She ran her fingers over a few blades of grass poking through the snow. She replayed the conversation with Grand Pabbie over and over in her head.

Grand Pabbie said polar bears spend most of their time drifting on ice floes, she thought. *He said polar bears travel long distances. He said they rarely, if ever, head south. How could the polar bears have traveled to Arendelle by mistake?* She rested her head against the tree and closed her eyes. Then she took a deep, calming breath.

CRASH!

Anna's eyes popped open. "What was that?" she said. She stood and walked to the edge of the cliff. She heard a low rumbling sound. She looked to her right just in time to see a large pile of snow slide off the mountain and tumble into the sea. *CRASH!*

Anna gazed down at the harbor, then farther out to sea. She scanned the horizon. She squinted and peered into the distance. Not an ice floe in sight.

That's odd, she thought. From this height, she could usually see hundreds of icebergs bobbing in the water. *I guess it* has *been a little warm lately. And Elin did mention that some of the ice in the harbor had thawed.*

Anna looked back at the cliff face. She watched as a few snow-covered rocks slid and crashed into the sea. Grand Pabbie's voice came back to her, reminding her that polar bears travel with the help of floating ice.

"I've got it!" she yelled triumphantly. She turned back to the forest and dashed toward the palace.

Anna raced across the royal gardens and burst through the palace doors. She walked quickly down the hall to the audience chamber, where Elsa and Olaf were waiting.

"Anna!" Elsa said, rising from her throne. "I was worried about you. You were gone a long time!" She threw her arms around her sister and gave her a tight squeeze.

"I'm sorry," Anna said. She patted Olaf's head and smiled. "I just needed some time to think. And guess what? I think I've finally figured out our polar bear problem!"

Anna explained to Elsa all she had seen at the bluff. She described the snow melting off the cliff faces and crashing into the fjord. She reported that there weren't any ice floes in the water. She reminded Elsa and Olaf what Elin had said about the thawing ice in the harbor. Finally, she recapped what Grand Pabbie had told them about the ways polar bears live.

"See, Elsa?" Anna said. "It all adds up!"

She pulled out her evidence notebook

and flipped through the pages. "Our polar bears were probably drifting on an ice floe, since that's what polar bears usually do. But for some reason, they drifted south instead of north."

Anna paused. She wanted to make sure Elsa was following her.

"Uh-huh," Olaf said, nodding. "Go on."

Anna continued. "By the time our bears reached the shores of Arendelle, this unusually warm weather we've been having must have melted their ice floe, stranding them here on the mainland."

Anna flipped the page and glanced at her notes. "With no way to get back home, and no food, the bears started stealing fish

from the wharf and pies from the bakery to survive. For our polar bears, the trash heap must have become a kind of home away from home."

Anna finished making her case and snapped her evidence book shut. She waited patiently for Elsa to take in this new information.

Elsa sat back down in her throne and rested her chin in her hand. After a few quiet moments, she spoke up.

"That's great work, Anna. We finally know how the polar bears got to Arendelle. What I'm not sure about, though, is how exactly we get them *home.*"

Anna smiled. "The same way they got here in the first place," she said. "Come on, Elsa. There's no time to lose. Let's go to the wharf."

Chapter 9

Anna and Elsa made their way along the waterfront to the Arendelle wharf. They passed stacks and stacks of wooden crates, towering coils of woven rope, and other fishing equipment. They trudged down the sloping banks of the harbor, all the way to the water's edge.

"This looks like a good spot," Anna

said, spreading her arms wide in the direction of the sea.

"A good spot for what?" Elsa asked. "I still don't understand what we're doing here."

Anna turned and smiled at her sister. "If the polar bears traveled all the way from the Arctic on an ice floe, than traveling on an ice floe is the way for them to get back, right?"

Elsa nodded. Anna continued.

"But Elin said there isn't any more ice in the harbor. There's no chance that our bears can climb on a iceberg and drift home, unless . . ."

Elsa laughed and smiled at Anna. "Unless I use my magic to make one."

"Exactly." Anna nodded.

"All right," Elsa said. "Let me handle this."

Elsa took a step forward and stretched her arms out in front of her. She took a deep breath. Then she looked over her shoulder and winked at her sister. "You might want to stand back for this one."

Anna took two giant steps backward. Meanwhile, Elsa closed her eyes and concentrated. An icy stream of wind swirled and spiraled above the bay. Elsa raised and lowered her hands. The dark water churned and gurgled. A moment later, Elsa dropped her hands to her side. A giant sheet of ice bobbed in the sea.

"Not bad, Elsa," Anna said with a

laugh. "I think that ought to do it."

"I hope so!" Elsa said, throwing her arms around her sister's neck. "Do you think the bears will have any trouble finding it?"

Anna looked at the perfectly formed ice floe. "They couldn't miss it," she said. "I bet those polar bears are eager to get back home."

Anna, feeling more confident than ever, took her sister's arm and happily marched to the palace.

*

The morning dawned still and fair in Arendelle. Birds were chirping. There wasn't a cloud in sight. But Anna stood at the water's edge, dumbfounded.

Elsa's magical ice floe was floating in the harbor in the exact same spot as the day before, with not so much as a paw print on it. Obviously, the polar bears were still hiding somewhere in town. Anna slumped down on a rusty old shrimp crate and sighed.

"So much for being eager to get home," Elsa said with a sympathetic shrug.

Anna smiled and hopped up from her crate. Now was not the time to give up! "Okay," she said, pacing the town dock. "We know that building an ice floe for the polar bears was the right idea. Maybe they just need some . . . encouragement?"

Elsa nodded. "We could lure them to

the glacier," she said. "With food, or—"

"Music!" Anna interjected. "Oh, Elsa, I can't believe it! This is just like the story I read to the village children."

Anna quickly told Elsa the story of the Pied Piper. She described how the rats of Hamelin had eaten all of the villagers' food and left piles of trash in their wake. Thanks to the Pied Piper and his magic flute, however, the villagers of Hamelin had been saved.

"So all we need to do is play a magic flute to lead the bears out of Arendelle?" Elsa asked. She looked doubtful.

"I know it sounds crazy," Anna said, "but think about it. What could possibly have attracted the bears to the village laundry? What does Leander always do while he works?"

Elsa scrunched her eyebrows, thinking. Suddenly, it hit her. "He hums!" she cried. "Maybe these polar bears *do* like music!"

"It's worth a shot," Anna said. "Come on!"

Anna and Elsa rushed from the wharf to the edge of the forest across town. They stopped for a moment to catch their breath. Then Elsa flicked her hands in the air and conjured a flute made entirely of solid ice.

"Here goes nothing," she said. She brought the ice flute to her mouth and blew.

Squawwwwwwk. Squawwwwk. Squawk.

Elsa lowered the flute and looked at it sideways. "What was *that*?"

Anna, meanwhile, was doubled over, hands on her knees, laughing. "Elsa, it sounds like a flock of geese when you play that thing!"

Elsa shook her head and tried again. She blew into the mouthpiece, but the squawking only sent Anna into another fit of laughter.

"I don't think this is going to help us lure the bears out of the forest," Elsa said. "This is worse than Kristoff's pots and pans!"

Anna lowered her hands from her ears, nodding. "That squawking has probably scared the bears away!" she said.

The sisters set off for the palace in search of a better instrument. As they approached the town square, however, Anna saw Olaf marching and dancing, his hands clasped around his carrot nose. He was playing a silly, catchy tune. The village children had fallen in line behind the snowman and were parading around the clock tower. Anna was reminded again of the story time she had hosted several days earlier. Olaf had performed a perfect imitation of the Pied Piper of Hamelin then, too.

Anna leaned close to Elsa and whispered, "I think we've found our Piper."

Elsa laughed. "Oh, Anna, I think we have, too."

Chapter 10

Olaf finished playing his piper song and stood in the center of the town square, waving goodbye to the children.

"See you later!" he called cheerfully.

Anna and Elsa tiptoed up behind him, clasping their hands behind their backs.

"Olaf . . . ?" Anna said innocently.

"Hi!" Olaf said, clapping his hands together. "Did you come for a warm hug?"

Anna and Elsa exchanged knowing glances. "Actually, Olaf," Elsa said, "Anna and I were just admiring your beautiful playing."

"You sound just how I imagine the Pied Piper of Hamelin would!" Anna exclaimed.

Olaf's face broke out in a shy smile. "That's so sweet." He dragged his foot across the snow, feeling bashful. "I *have* been practicing."

"That's wonderful, Olaf," Elsa said.

Anna knelt in the snowy grass and made a very serious face. "Olaf, would you like the chance to become a *real* Pied Piper?"

Olaf looked at Anna in surprise and awe. "Yes," he said.

Anna and Elsa led Olaf out of the village, across the clearing, and to the edge of the forest. Olaf chattered the whole way.

"This is so exciting!" he said, waving his stick arms with enthusiasm. "I can't believe I'm going to be a real Pied Piper. I wonder what kind of music polar bears like. Should I play something up-tempo?"

"You'll be great, Olaf," Anna said, patting the snowman's head. "Just play the way you usually do."

The friends came to a stop at the forest tree line and pricked their ears. It was eerily silent. Anna could feel the sun's strong rays warming her arms and face.

"All right, Olaf. You can do this," she told him.

Olaf gave Anna and Elsa a confident nod. Then he grabbed his carrot nose with both hands and began to play, softly at first, then louder and louder. Before long, Anna heard the rustling of leaves in the forest.

"Do you hear that, Elsa?" Anna whispered. She turned her face toward the trees. She could just make out the sound of limbs snapping and breaking.

"Keep going, Olaf!" Elsa said.

Olaf continued stomping and marching to the music. After a few moments, he dropped his stick arms from his carrot nose completely. His voice rang out at full volume. He sang and waved his stick arms with glee.

Anna heard another rustle of leaves. She looked at the forest just as three furry white heads poked out between the trees.

"Anna! I think it's working!" Elsa whispered, clasping her hands beneath her chin.

Anna watched as the mama polar bear trotted out from the woods and into the clearing, followed by the two adorable cubs. Instead of snarling or rearing up on her hind legs, however, the mama bear placidly moved her head back and forth. She seemed to be enjoying Olaf's song.

Anna reached for Elsa's hand just as Olaf took an unscheduled break from his music. "Oh, look at them," he said, admiring the bears. "They're so majestic."

Suddenly, the mama bear shook her head from side to side. She narrowed her eyes and started to growl.

"Olaf!" Anna cried out. "Don't stop!"

Olaf grabbed his nose and began to play again, and the mama bear and her cubs fell in line behind him once more. They took another step forward with every note of Olaf's song.

"Okay, Olaf," Anna whispered. "We need to lead the bears back through town, all the way to the wharf. Think you can do that?"

Olaf continued to play, but he managed to give Anna a reassuring wink. He walked backward through the clearing, placing one foot cautiously behind the other. The bears slowly followed him. Anna and Elsa followed at a safe distance.

Olaf merrily led the three bears toward town. He slid down a snowy hill, and the cubs followed playfully. The snowman didn't stop playing the whole time.

The streets of Arendelle echoed with the glorious sound of Olaf's nose song. Curious villagers threw open their windows and filed out of their homes to get a better view of the impromptu parade. Anna followed Olaf and the bears, clapping in time to the beat. She turned her head when she heard a whistle ring out from the side of the street.

It was Kristoff, leaning against the wall of Leander's laundry. He cupped his hands around his mouth and hollered over the crowd, "Nice work, Anna!"

Anna smiled and waved.

Olaf marched along the wharf, all the way to the end of the town dock. To Anna's delight, the polar bears suddenly jumped into the water and dog-paddled out to the ice floe Elsa had made.

"Way to go, Olaf!" Elsa said. She stretched out her arm and an icy wind swirled out over the harbor. The ice floe began to drift northward, carrying the polar bears to their Arctic home.

The villagers of Arendelle broke into

spontaneous clapping and cheers. "Three cheers for the Polar Bear Piper!" someone cried.

Olaf, delighted by all the attention, continued to play his beautiful song. Some of the villagers formed a circle around him, clapping and dancing in the middle of the town square. Anna and Elsa looked at each other and beamed with pride.

Just then, two villagers stepped forward. Anna recognized them from the day everyone had pitched in to help clean up the garbage heap. One was a craftsman. The other was one of the village's hardest-working farmers.

"Queen Elsa, Princess Anna," the

craftsman said with a bow. "In honor of your help solving our polar bear problem, the people of Arendelle would like to present you with these gifts."

The craftsman held up a beautiful new vase that had been made entirely from glass shards recycled from the trash pile.

Elsa held the vase high in the air to admire it. It glittered in the sun. "Who knew that trash could be turned into such treasure?" she said.

Next, the farmer stepped forward. He held aloft a basket filled with fruits and vegetables.

"Thank you for the compost, Princess Anna," the farmer said with a smile.

As Anna reached out to accept the basket, Sven suddenly lunged forward and took a bite out of a giant carrot. Kristoff, slightly embarrassed, covered his face with his hand and shook his head.

"Don't worry, Sven," Anna whispered to the reindeer. "You've earned it."

Sven nuzzled her in appreciation.

Anna was looking out at the happy villagers, all of them singing and dancing to Olaf's tune, when she felt Elsa's arm wrap around her shoulders.

"Well, the polar bear problem is finally solved," Elsa said. "I wonder, what do you think Nansina Drude would do now?"

Anna laughed out loud. "Oh, Elsa,"

she said, "I think she'd take a very long winter's nap!"

"Me too," Elsa said, hugging her sister. "Come on, Anna. Let's go home."

Erica David has written more than forty books and comics for young readers, including Marvel Adventures *Spider-Man: The Sinister Six.* She graduated from Princeton University and is an MFA candidate at the Writer's Foundry in Brooklyn. She has always had an interest in all things magical, fantastic, and frozen, which has led her to work for Nickelodeon, Marvel, and an ice cream parlor, respectively. She resides sometimes in Philadelphia and sometimes in New York, with a canine familiar named Skylar.